The Dragonsitter to the Rescue

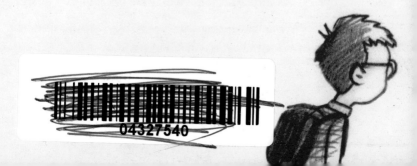

First published in 2016 by
Andersen Press Limited
20 Vauxhall Bridge Road
London SW1V 2SA
www.andersenpress.co.uk

2 4 6 8 10 9 7 5 3 1

British Library Cataloguing in Publication Data available.

ISBN 978 1 78344 329 1

Printed and bound by CPI Group
(UK) Ltd, Croydon, CR0 4YY

The Dragonsitter to the Rescue

Josh Lacey

Illustrated by Garry Parsons

Andersen Press
London

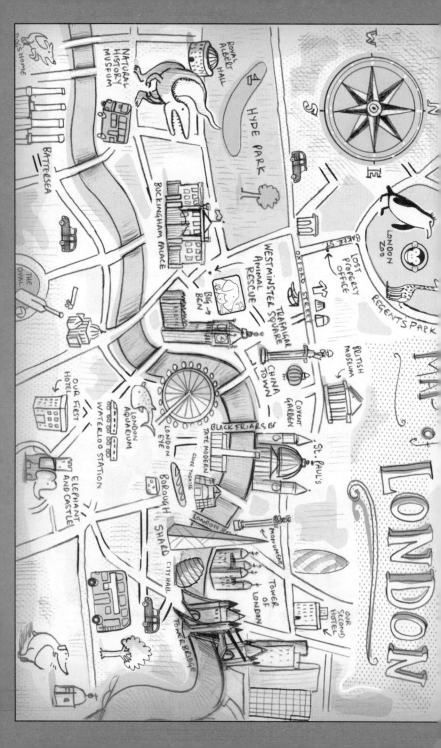

Dear Uncle Morton

Here is the view from our hotel window. If you look very closely, you can see Big Ben.

As you can also see, your dragons are fine.
They both had a good supper. Now they're
fast asleep.

Dad didn't actually want to bring them.
He asked Mum to take them to Paris, but
she said, "No way." She said she didn't want
two badly-behaved dragons spoiling her
romantic weekend with Gordon.

Dad said wasn't a romantic weekend in Paris a bit of a cliché, and Mum said she'd rather have a cliché than nothing at all, which was all *he* used to give her.

Gordon looked really embarrassed while they were shouting at one another, but Emily and I didn't mind. We're used to it.

Mum won. So the dragons are here. I have brought the egg too just in case it hatches. I wouldn't want a new dragon to arrive in an empty house.

I have to go now. Dad says it's bedtime. First thing tomorrow morning we're visiting the Natural History Museum.

Emily wants to go on the London Eye instead, but Dad says we'll do that the day after.

I hope you're having fun in Tibet. Have you seen the yeti yet?

Love from

Eddie

Dear Uncle Morton

I have to tell you some bad news.

We have lost Arthur.

He's somewhere in London, but I don't know where.

Today we went to the Natural History Museum. I've always wanted to go there, so I was *really* excited.

The only problem was Dad said the dragons had to stay in the hotel without us.

I said that was very unfair, but Dad said he wanted to spend some quality time with his children, not a pair of fire-breathing lizards. He said we could take them to a park later if they needed to stretch their wings.

He absolutely definitely no-question-about-it refused to change his mind.

So I hid Arthur in my backpack.

I knew I shouldn't, but I couldn't stop myself.

I told him to be quiet in there. He *was*, on the tube. Very. And he carried on being quiet in the cafe where we stopped for elevenses. I dropped some croissant through the top of the backpack, which seemed to keep him happy.

He even stayed quiet in the museum. He didn't make a squeak while we looked at the birds and the bears and the earthworms and the giraffe and the rhino and the dodo and the dolphin and the blue whale.

But when we got to the T-Rex, he wriggled out of my backpack and flew off to have a look. Maybe he thought it was a long-lost relation.

He flew the entire length of the T-Rex from tail to head and landed on its nostrils. People were pointing and shouting and taking pictures.

Dad said, "Where did that come from?"

I pretended I didn't know.

Guards came running. One of them said, "You're not allowed flying toys inside the museum."

I explained, "He's not a toy, he's a dragon."

The guard said he didn't care what it was, I just had to get it out of here right now this minute before he called the police and had us all ejected for making a public nuisance of ourselves.

I said I would if I could catch him.

The guard got on his walkie-talkie and called for reinforcements.

Unfortunately catching Arthur was easier said than done. He jumped off the T-Rex

and whooshed over our heads, waggling his wings.

I ran after him. So did Dad and Emily and lots of guards.

Arthur was faster than any of us. He flew along the corridors, looped the loop around some statues, dive-bombed a crowd of Japanese tourists and disappeared through the revolving doors. By the time we got outside, he had disappeared.

We searched for hours, but we couldn't find him anywhere.

I wanted to carry on looking all night, but Dad said we'd just be wasting our time. So we came back to the hotel.

Ziggy was fast asleep. She still is. I don't know what I'm going to say to her when she wakes up.

Dad says if I was so concerned about the dragons, I shouldn't have hidden Arthur in my backpack in the first place. I suppose he's right.

I'm really sorry, Uncle Morton.

This whole thing is my fault, and I wish I knew how to make it better.

Eddie

From: Edward Smith–Pickle

To: Morton Pickle

Date: Sunday 16 April

Subject: More bad news

Attachments: Into the night

Dear Uncle Morton

I'm very sorry, but I've got some more bad news.

I've lost your other dragon too.

Emily and I were cleaning our teeth in the bathroom when we heard a terrible racket coming from the bedroom.

We rushed out of the bathroom and found Ziggy going wild. She was trying to break through the windows and get onto the balcony. She must have realised Arthur had gone missing.

Dad was standing on his bed, holding a pillow. He yelled at me to do something.

I didn't want to let her out, but there really wasn't any choice. One more minute and she would have smashed the whole place to pieces.

So I opened the door.

Ziggy charged onto the balcony, flapped her wings and took off.

A moment later she'd disappeared into the night.

I feel awful. I can't believe I've lost both your dragons. I wish I knew how to find them.

Do you have any brilliant ideas?

Dad says there's no point writing to you because you won't be checking your emails in Tibet, but I hope you get this message.

Please write back if you do.

Eddie

Dear Uncle Morton

Your dragons are still missing.

We spent the whole day walking round London, but we didn't see any sign of them.

This city is so big!

Dad says eight million people live here. I think we met most of them.

I asked everyone if they'd seen a missing dragon. Some of them laughed. Others just walked past as if they couldn't even hear me.

People who live in London are quite rude. Dad says it's the same in all big cities. Emily wanted to know if Paris is like this too, and Dad said it's even worse.

I hope Mum and Gordon are having more fun than us.

Love from

Eddie

Dear Uncle Morton

We spent today searching for your dragons again, but we still haven't found them.

Dad says not to worry and they'll come back in their own good time.

He says this is our one chance to spend a few days in London and we should be making the most of it, missing dragons or no missing dragons.

But I don't want to make the most of it. I just want to find Ziggy and Arthur.

Eddie

Dear Eddie

I have just seen your messages. The internet is a rare treat here in Tibet, but I managed to check my emails on a sherpa's phone.

Thank you for letting me know about the dragons.

You needn't worry about Ziggy. She will be perfectly safe. Dragons are wise creatures, and she is even more sensible than most. She also has strong wings and powerful claws. I can't imagine anyone or anything in London will be a threat to her.

However, Arthur is quite different, and I am very concerned for his safety. A small dragon is not safe alone in a big city. He might have been run over, or kidnapped, or suffered some even more horrible fate.

17

I suggest you call the police and ask for their help.

I do hope you find them both soon, so you can enjoy your holiday in London. I have fond memories of the years I spent in that vast grey town. Few places could be more different than my current location, a cold snow-covered mountainside in a remote region of Tibet.

We have had no confirmed sightings of the yeti, but I have arranged a meeting with a local shaman tomorrow, and I am hoping he will bring good news.

With love from

Your affectionate uncle

Morton

From: Edward Smith-Pickle

To: Morton Pickle

Date: Wednesday 19 April

Subject: Police

Dear Uncle Morton

I did what you suggested.

I called the police and told them we had lost a dragon in the Natural History Museum.

First the policeman thought I was joking.

Then he said he would arrest me for wasting police time.

Do you have any other suggestions for finding Arthur?

Eddie

Dear Uncle Morton

Your dragons are still missing.

Dad says he's had quite enough of them, even if they're not here any more, and we should just concentrate on enjoying what little time we have left in London.

But I can't make the most of anything because I'm too worried about Ziggy and Arthur.

I made some posters and pinned them to trees.

No one has replied yet, but I hope they will soon.

Love from

Eddie

Have you seen this dragon?

He is small and green.

He has two wings and smoke coming out of his nostrils.

He was last seen on Sunday 16 April in the Natural History Museum.

If you see him, please contact Eddie.

edwardsmithpickle@gmail.com

From: Edward Smith–Pickle

To: Morton Pickle

Date: Thursday 20 April

Subject: Noodles

Attachments: Gerrard Street

Dear Uncle Morton

We have been looking for your dragons again today.

We didn't find them.

We did see some other dragons, but not yours.

Dad's friend Julie came to have lunch with us. She's really pretty like all his girlfriends.

Dad said she's not actually his girlfriend, but fingers crossed. I hope she will be. She was very nice.

Also she knows a lot about dragons.

She took us to Chinatown because she said they have hundreds of dragons there. She was right. There were dragons everywhere.

Unfortunately none of them were Arthur or Ziggy. But we did have some delicious noodles.

I put up some more posters. I still haven't had any replies.

Love from

Eddie

From: Edward Smith-Pickle

To: Morton Pickle

Date: Friday 21 April

Subject: She's back!

📎 **Attachments:** A very tired dragon

Dear Uncle Morton

I have some good news and some bad news.

The good news is Ziggy is back.

The bad news is Arthur isn't.

Ziggy must have arrived in the middle of the night. She's asleep on the balcony. I suppose she was exhausted from searching so much. In a minute I'm going to wake her up to say hello. Then we're going to spend the day searching for Arthur. Julie is going to come with us. She's taken the day off work.

Dad said couldn't we do something more interesting than looking for Arthur? But I said we've got to find him.

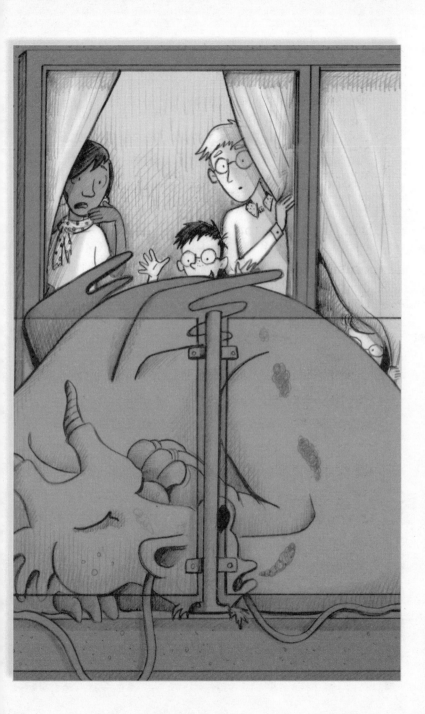

Also Julie won't mind. She loves dragons. She told me so yesterday.

Emily said maybe we would be able to see Arthur from the top of the London Eye, but I know she didn't really mean it. She just wants to go up there herself.

I told her there would be time to enjoy ourselves after we've found him.

Love from

Eddie

From: Edward Smith-Pickle

To: Morton Pickle

Date: Friday 21 April

Subject: Fizz

Attachments: Cheers!; Shower

Dear Uncle Morton

We are cold and wet and homeless, and it's all your dragon's fault.

We spent today searching for Arthur, but we didn't find him.

Julie took us to Covent Garden and Trafalgar Square and the National Gallery, which were all very nice, but I didn't enjoy them much because I was too worried about Arthur.

So Dad said tonight as a special treat to cheer ourselves up we could have room service and watch a movie in bed. He invited Julie to join us, but she was busy.

27

Once we got back to the hotel, Emily and I had a bath and put on our PJs, then switched on the telly. Dad ordered burgers and chips plus lemonade for me and orange for Emily and a bottle of red wine for him.

I wanted to get a drink for Ziggy, but Dad said she'd be fine with water.

We had just started watching the movie when the waiter arrived with our supper on a big silver tray.

Dad poured himself a big drink and stretched out on the bed and said, "Cheers." We all clinked glasses.

I felt a bit guilty about Arthur. You know how much he loves chips. Also I didn't like having fun while he was missing. Dad told me not to worry.

He said, "Look at Ziggy. She's enjoying herself, isn't she?" And he was right. She was.

She ate her burger in one gulp, and her chips in another. Then she ate most of mine too.

Unfortunately she also drank my lemonade.

I didn't see her doing it, but she must have swallowed the lot because suddenly she did an enormous burp.

Flames shot across the room. A corner of the duvet caught fire.

Dad jumped off the bed and grabbed the fire extinguisher. He was just working out how to turn it on when the fire alarm went off.

It was the loudest noise I've ever heard. Until Emily screamed.

Ziggy didn't seem too bothered by all the fuss. She just reached across the bed and grabbed the remains of our burgers.

I was suggesting everyone should calm down when the sprinklers started. It was like standing under a waterfall. In seconds we were all soaked to the skin.

Now we're waiting in the car park in our wet pyjamas while the firemen check all the rooms.

Dad is talking to the people who own the hotel. They want us to leave immediately, but we don't have anywhere to go.

Dad says the whole thing is your stupid dragon's fault and if you had a scrap of decency you'd come straight back from Tibet and look after her yourself.

I thought you probably couldn't do that, Uncle Morton.

But do you think maybe you could?

Eddie

From: Edward Smith–Pickle
To: Morton Pickle
Date: Friday 21 April
Subject: Hotel Hoxton

Dear Uncle Morton

Don't worry about coming back from Tibet. Everything is fine. We're in a new hotel.

It's quite nice here. The TV in the room is even bigger than the last one and they left two free chocolates on our pillows.

Ziggy seems to like it too. She ate both the chocolates, then fell asleep on the carpet.

I don't know why she isn't more worried about Arthur. Perhaps she's forgotten all about him. Dad said some mothers are like that.

She's actually very lucky to be here at all. There was a big sign outside the hotel which said NO PETS ALLOWED.

Dad asked if they could make an exception for dragons.

They laughed and said dragons could stay free of charge, which was very nice of them.

They tried to change their minds when they saw Ziggy, but Dad said a deal is a deal, so they let us all in.

There's only one problem. Arthur doesn't know where we are. If he goes to the other hotel, he won't be able to find us.

Do you think I should go back there and wait for him?

Eddie

Dear Uncle Morton

Today is our last day in London.

We're going home tomorrow.

There's still no sign of Arthur.

I want to stay here till we find him, but Dad says that's just not possible. Apparently this hotel is costing him an arm and a leg. Also we have school next week and he has to go back to Wales.

Dad said how would we like to spend our last day in London?

I said I wanted to look for Arthur. Emily said she wanted to go to the London Eye.

Dad said we've been looking for Arthur

every day this week and it was about time we did something a bit more interesting, so we're going to the London Eye.

Apparently Julie has never been on it, even though she's lived in London her whole life.

Emily can't stop smiling. I don't know why. Doesn't she even care about your dragon?

I can't believe we're wasting our last day sightseeing when we could be looking for Arthur.

But no one is taking any notice of me.

Eddie

From: Edward Smith-Pickle

To: Morton Pickle

Date: Saturday 22 April

Subject: Good news!!!!!!

Attachments: Transport for London Report

Dear Uncle Morton

We have found Arthur!

Well, we've almost found him.

We know where he is, anyway.

Today we went on the London Eye. I didn't really want to be there, but it was actually quite amazing. From the top we could see the whole city.

I looked in every direction, but I couldn't see any dragons.

When we came down again, Julie had a chat with one of the guards, who suggested we try the Lost Property Office at Baker Street Station. He said lost things in London often end up there.

He was right!

We took the tube to Baker Street and talked to the Duty Officer at the Lost Property Office. He said maybe he could help us.

He looked through his files and pulled out a piece of paper and said, "Does this sound like what you're looking for?"

Unfortunately Arthur wasn't there any more. He's been taken away by the Westminster Animal Rescue Service.

Dad said they're welcome to him. But he was only joking.

We're going there now to get him back.

Eddie

Lost Property Office, Baker Street Station

Item

One creature. Species unknown. Small, green, possibly dangerous.

Location

The item was found on a Circle Line train travelling clockwise between Gloucester Road and High Street Kensington.

Description

At approximately 8 p.m. last night, a passenger boarded a Circle Line train at Gloucester Road and noticed the item on the next seat. The carriage was not crowded and there was no sign of an owner nearby.

The passenger alerted a member of staff, who summoned the British Transport Police. They placed the item in a cardboard box and brought it to the Lost Property Office at Baker Street.

The Duty Officer examined the creature, but could not find a collar or any evidence of a microchip.

However the creature does possess very sharp teeth, which it has already used to bite two Transport for London staff members. Luckily both of them were wearing thick boots.

The Lost Property Office has very limited provision for livestock or pets, so the Duty Officer placed the item in the Umbrella Room for safekeeping.

I have reported the matter to the Westminster Animal Rescue Service. I hope they will arrive soon. The item has already destroyed six umbrellas and is currently working its way through a seventh.

Andy Malik

Andy Malik, Deputy Duty Officer, Baker Street Lost Property Office

From: Edward Smith-Pickle

To: Morton Pickle

Date: Saturday 22 April

Subject: Your overgrown newt

Attachments: WAR Report

Dear Uncle Morton

The Westminster Animal Rescue Service don't have Arthur any more. They've taken him to the Zoo.

We're on our way.

Love from

Eddie

The Westminster Animal Rescue Service

Report by Monika Pielowska, Senior Warden

I was contacted by the Deputy Duty Officer in Baker Street Station, who informed me of a situation at the Transport for London Lost Property Office. I was at an address nearby, so I made my way directly to Baker Street.

The Duty Officer told me that a small creature, species unknown, was handed in last night and placed in the Umbrella Room.

The Duty Officer claimed that the creature was extremely dangerous, although it seemed perfectly harmless to me.

The creature does have very sharp teeth and an unusual habit of breathing smoke through its nostrils.

One of the Duty Officers suggested it might be a dragon, but I assured him that such things do not exist. I am not an expert on lizards, but it looks to me like an overgrown newt.

Whatever it might be, the creature was clearly very hungry. It had already tried to eat every umbrella in the place, without much success. So I tempted it into a cage with a bait of raw steak.

Once it was safely locked inside the cage, I carried the creature to my van and conveyed it to London Zoo, where it will be properly identified by an expert.

Dear Uncle Morton

We've found Arthur! He's in the Zoo.

The only problem is they won't let him go.

They want proof we are his registered owners. Do you have any proof, Uncle Morton?

If so, please send it to us ASAP. Otherwise Arthur will be sent to another zoo for tests, and then how are we supposed to get him back?

Love from

Eddie

The Zoological Society of London

NEW ADMISSION INFORMATION SHEET

Species: Unknown.

Habitat: Unknown.

Diet: Unknown.

Sex: Unknown.

Age: Unknown.

Previous owner: Unknown.

Place of origin: the Circle Line.

Notes: Three of our foremost lizard experts have examined this unusual creature, trying to determine its species, but they remain baffled.

One of them suggested it may be a rare form of the Jamaican Chameleon. Another has agreed to consult his colleagues at the Taronga Zoo in Sydney. The third suffered minor burns and is currently at the A&E department of the Royal Free Hospital. The creature has not been disturbed again.

It will be tranquilised on Monday morning and transferred to Whipsnade Zoo for further examination.

From: Edward Smith–Pickle

To: Morton Pickle

Date: Sunday 23 April

Subject: The Zoo

Attachments: Picnic; Take–off; Gorillas; Cages

Dear Uncle Morton

Don't worry about sending the proof. We've got Arthur. We rescued him ourselves.

Actually Ziggy did. She was amazing!

We were meant to be going straight home today, but I said couldn't we go to the Zoo on our way, and Dad said if we had to.

I think he was just sad because Julie isn't coming with us. She went to have Sunday lunch with her mum and dad in Ipswich, and we weren't invited.

Dad doesn't know when he's going to see her again.

I said why doesn't he invite her to stay in Wales, and he said maybe he will.

Anyway, we packed our bags and checked out of the hotel. They gave us some more chocolates as a going-home present. Then Dad drove us to the Zoo.

It's in the middle of a nice park. That was where Dad made us wait while he talked to whoever was in charge.

We had to promise not to move an inch. And we didn't. While Dad went into the Zoo, we sat on the grass, eating chocolates.

Suddenly Ziggy lifted her head into the air and looked around. Somehow she must have sensed Arthur was nearby.

She flapped her wings.

Faster and faster.

Just before she took off, I jumped on her back.

Emily was shouting at me to get off. She grabbed Ziggy's tail and clung on.

With one shake Ziggy sent her flying across the grass. Then she flapped her wings again and we were in the air.

All around the park I could see people shouting and pointing at us. I wanted to wave back, but I knew what would happen if I let go.

The Zoo is surrounded by a huge metal fence covered with spikes and prickles. That didn't stop Ziggy. She just flew over the top and swept past the cages.

The animals went wild.

Parrots shrieked. Monkeys screamed. The lions threw back their heads and roared, telling us to get lost.

Only the gorillas wanted to stand and fight.
They ran across the grass into the middle
of their enclosure and beat their fists
against their chests.

Ziggy ignored them all. She just flew this way and that, following her nose, searching for Arthur.

Suddenly she flipped around in mid-air and headed for some grey buildings at the back of the Zoo where visitors aren't even allowed.

Ziggy seemed to know exactly where she was going. She flew straight towards a big window on the fifth floor. On the other side of the glass, I could see a room filled with about twenty cages, each of them holding a different animal. There was a monkey and a chimp and a wolf and a marmoset and a goose and a small dragon, all going wild, beating their paws and their claws against the bars.

Ziggy breathed a great gust of fire and the glass exploded. Another gust and the bars melted on half the cages.

The wolf howled. The monkey lost his eyebrows. The goose almost went up in flames.

Arthur took off. He sped across the floor and through the window, his little wings flapping like a hummingbird's. Then he landed beside me on his mum's back.

Through the window I could see a zookeeper staring at us, his mouth wide open, his clothes smoking.

I wanted to say sorry, but there wasn't time before Ziggy whirled around and flew across the Zoo.

The gorillas went wild again. The lions roared. I could see all the penguins staring up at us, and the giraffes too. I would have liked to dive down and have a better look, but Ziggy wanted to get out of there ASAP.

She soared over the fence and plunged down to land on the grass beside Emily.

Dad was already running towards us. He must have seen what was happening. He bundled us into the car and we drove straight home.

When we got here, Arthur ate seven sausages, two jacket potatoes and half a bar of Dairy Milk, then fell asleep in front of the telly.

I think he's going to be fine.

Dad has gone back to Wales. He says next time he'd rather it was just us and no dragons. Maybe they could stay with Mum and Gordon instead.

Love from

Eddie

From: Morton Pickle

To: Edward Smith-Pickle

Date: Monday 24 April

Subject: Re: The Zoo

Dear Eddie

What wonderful news about Arthur!

Congratulations on rescuing him from the Zoo. It's actually extremely fortunate that you did, because I don't have any proof that I own him.

In fact, I don't own him. Nor do I own Ziggy. Dragons are not like dogs, cats, gerbils, or any other ordinary pet. They cannot really have an owner because they own themselves. Ziggy and Arthur are simply staying with me until they decide to move elsewhere.

All is well here in Tibet. I am currently staying in a village high in the Himalayas. We still do not have a confirmed sighting of the yeti, but today we did find what might

53

have been one of his footprints in the snow. We are going to search for him again first thing tomorrow morning.

I'm so pleased that the dragons are in such good hands while I'm away. Thanks again for looking after them so well.

With love from

your affectionate uncle

Morton

Dear Uncle Morton

Will you please send me some pictures of the footprints? I've always wanted to see a yeti.

If you find one, will you bring it home? Do you think it will make friends with the dragons?

They're both fine, by the way.

We had fish fingers for tea. Arthur ate seven, and Ziggy had nine. Now they're dozing in front of the telly.

Mum would like to know when you're planning to come and collect them. She says it's very nice having the dragons to stay, but she'd quite like to have the house to herself again.

I think she's just feeling a bit grumpy because Gordon's gone home. Apparently they had the best time ever in Paris.

Emily asked if we could go too next time, and Mum said, "We'll see."

I'm feeling a bit grumpy too, because I had to go back to school today.

It was OK, but being on holiday was much more fun.

Love from

Eddie

PS The egg still hasn't hatched. I've put it back in my sock drawer for now.

GREETINGS
FROM TIBET

Dear Eddie

Yesterday we spotted
a yeti!

We are going after him
today.

Love from

Uncle Morton

Eddie

29 Po

Sh

U

The Dragonsitter's Island

Josh Lacey

Illustrated by Garry Parsons

Dear Uncle Morton,
The McDougalls are here. Mr McDougall won't stop
shouting and waving his arms. He has lost three sheep
in a week. Now he wants to take your dragons away
and lock them in his barn till the police arrive.

Eddie is dragonsitting on Uncle Morton's Scottish
island. But something is eating the local sheep.
Can Eddie find the real culprit?

Praise for *The Dragonsitter*:
'Ideal for young readers,
and belly-busting laughter
for all the family'
We Love This Book

9781783440450 £4.99

The Dragonsitter's Party

Josh Lacey

Illustrated by Garry Parsons

Dear Uncle Morton
Can you come to my birthday party? It's going to be great.
We're having a magician. Mum says your dragons aren't
invited, but you can take some cake home for them.

It's Eddie's birthday and he's looking forward to a birthday
party filled with fun, games and . . . dragons?
Ziggy and Arthur are the unexpected guests, but their
idea of a good time involves eating everything in sight
and ruining the party magician's tricks.
Is Eddie in for the wrong kind of
birthday surprise?

Praise for *The Dragonsitter*:
'Josh Lacey's comic timing
is impeccable'
Books for Keeps

9781783442294   £4.99